This book belongs to:

_____

_____

To my little cousin Christine.

- P.A.

To my friend Narizumi,
who introduced me
to manga oh so long ago.

- O.C.

To all the hard working Japanese
artists in the manga and anime
industry, my kid Agustin, and
nephew Mateo.

- J.C.

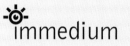

inspiring a world of imagination

Immedium, Inc.
P.O. Box 31846
San Francisco, CA 94131
www.immedium.com

www.liberumdonum.com

Text Copyright © 2019 Phil Amara and Oliver Chin

Illustrations Copyright © 2019 Juan Calle

First hardcover edition published 2019.

Edited by Don Menn
Book design by Joy Liu-Trujillo
Translation by Hiroko Amara

Printed in Malaysia
10 9 8 7 6 5 4 3 2 1

Library of Congress Cataloging-in-Publication Data

Names: Amara, Philip, author. | Chin, Oliver Clyde, 1969- author. | Calle,
Juan, 1977- illustrator.

Title: The discovery of anime and manga / by Phil Amara & Oliver Chin ;
illustrated by Juan Calle.

Description: First hardcover edition. | San Francisco : Immedium, Inc., 2019. | Series: The Asian hall of fame | Summary: "Dao, a red panda, guides
Ethan and Emma, two school children, back into time to discover how Japanese animation and comics were created and became popular worldwide"--
Provided by publisher.

Identifiers: LCCN 2019000143 (print) | LCCN 2019002950 (ebook) | ISBN 9781597021487 (e-book) | ISBN 9781597021463 (hardcover)
Subjects: | CYAC: Time travel--Fiction. | Comic books, strips, etc.--Fiction. | Animated films--Fiction. | Red panda--Fiction. | Japan--History--Fiction.
Classification: LCC PZ7.A49153 (ebook) | LCC PZ7.A49153 Dig 2019 (print) | DDC [E]--dc23

LC record available at https://lccn.loc.gov/2019000143

ISBN: 978-1-59702-146-3

The Discovery of
ANIME & MANGA
The Asian Hall of Fame

発見アニメまんがの世界

immedium

Immedium, Inc.
San Francisco, CA

by Phil Amara & Oliver Chin

Illustrated by Juan Calle

Ethan and Emma saw a colorful crowd headed to the convention center.
"This looks fun," said Ethan.

"Let's check it out," suggested Emma.
Once inside, they could hardly believe their eyes.

コンベンションセンターへと人の波が、続いている。
「おもしろそうだね」と、イーサン。

「行ってみよう」と、エマ。中に入って、二人は、びっくり。

Asian comic books featured a rainbow of characters.
"I want to write stories like these!" said Emma.

すてきなキャラクターが登場する、数多くのまんが。
「わたしも、こんなお話を書いてみたいわ」と、エマが言った。

イーサンも、「うわぁ、すごい。
こんな絵をかいてみたいな」
と、ため息。「ぼくが、
教えてあげるよ！」と、
聞いたことのあるやさしい声が、した。

Fantastic cartoons played with sensational action.
"I want to draw those!" shouted Ethan.

"I can show you," said a kind voice.

It was Dao You! This special red panda had taught them about ramen and fireworks.

"The Japanese word for comics is *manga*. Animation is *anime*," he explained.
"Do you want to learn how they were created?"

ダオ！前にもラーメンや花火のことを教えてくれた、
あのレッサーパンダのダオが、やってきた。

「まんがやアニメのこと、もっと、知りたいかい？」

"Sure!" they replied.

"The history of how Japan's popular culture changed the world is amazing,"
said Dao. By banging his small gong, he could transport them
to a distant place and time. "So let's go!" Gooone!

「うん、知りたい」と、二人は、答えた。「日本のポップカルチャーは、海外でもすごく、人気があるんだよ」
ダオは、そう言うと、小さなドラを鳴らした。「さあ、行こう！」 ゴーン！

'Welcome to the 12th century!" announced Dao. "In the old capital Nara, Buddhists practiced *e-toki*, or 'telling a story from a scroll.'"

「12世紀へようこそ」と、ダオの声。「昔、都があった奈良 では、

『絵 とき』が、おこなわれていたんだ。 絵ときっていうのは、おぼうさんが、

ぶっ教 の教えをわかりやすく絵を使って説明

してくれることだよ」

"It is like a cartoon," observed Emma.
"Smaller scenes in the painting
combine to tell a larger tale."

Zoom! They appeared in 1840 in Tokyo. "*Manga* means 'playful drawings,'" read Emma.

"That's what *these* are," remarked Ethan.

「うんうん。そういう感じがする」と、イーサン。ジャーン！ここは、1840年の東京。
「まんがには、『気の向くままにかいた絵』という意味があるみたい」
と、エマが、本を見ながら、イーサンに話しかけている。

"Hokusai was a famous painter," Dao said. "Prints of
his art were bound into books that became bestsellers."

浮世絵師 として有名な葛飾北斎は、こういうスケッチをたくさんかいていて、
それを集めた本が、当時ベストセラーになったんだよ」と、ダオが説明する。

They zipped to Osaka in 1935. Dao explained,
"Traveling storytellers carried *kamishibai*, large pictures displayed in a wooden box."

次に、ダオたちがやってきたのは、1935年の大阪。

「大きな箱を自転車に乗せて町のあちこちを回り、楽しい紙しばいを見せてくれるよ」

"I see!" said Ethan. "When the performer shows another illustration, the audience hears the next part of the story."

「なるほど！紙を引きぬきながら、お話を読んでいくんだね」と、イーサン。

They whisked ahead to 1945.

1945年。

Dao whispered, "However, during World War II,
the government rationed paper, banned manga,
and hired artists to make posters and cartoons
that supported their empire."

「まんがは、戦争中
プロパガンダとして利用されたこともあったよ」

"After the war, like many nations, Japan had to rebuild," said Dao.

「戦後、日本も他国と同じように、国を立て直していったよ。

"The US occupied Japan until 1952, and American culture was very influential.
Osamu Tezuka studied to be a doctor but became an artist."

日本は、1952年までアメリカのせんりょう下 にあって、アメリカ文化からさまざまな、
えいきょうを受けたよ」「手塚は、医者になる勉強をしながら、まんがをかいていたんだ」

Tezuka serialized his comic strips in many monthly magazines at the same time. He was so busy that he started his own studio. A manager handled his business while many assistants finished his drawings' details.

Called the "God of Manga," Tezuka loved seeing and producing films too.
He created a robot boy, a white lion cub, a mysterious doctor, and many more.
In his lifetime, he drew 150,000 pages and created 60 anime.

「『まんがの神様』とよばれた手塚は、アニメーションのせい作 にも力を注いだ。『鉄腕 アトム』、
『ジャングル大帝 』、『ブラック・ジャック』といったヒット作を生み出したんだ。
150,000まいをこえる、まんがをかき、60作もの、アニメをせい作したよ」

GIGANTOR

Zap! The trio were in the 1960s. "Now everyone wanted to watch TV," said Dao. "Anime was more than superheroes." One of the first anime broadcast in the US, *Tetsujin 28* is a gigantic robot controlled by a boy."

えーい！1960年代にタイムスリップ。「みんなが、テレビを見る時代が来たんだ」「『鉄人28号』は、アメリカで、はじめて放送_{ほう}されたアニメの一つ。男の子が、リモコンですきなロボットをそうじゅうするという話さ。

"*Speed Racer* is an 18-year-old who wants to be the best, pro, racecar driver," said Emma.

他にも、少年のレーサーとしての成長 をえがく
『マッハGoGoGo』や、

SPRITLE

CHIM CHIM

MACH 5

TRIXIE

SPEED RACER

SHIZUKA

DORAEMON

NOBITA

JIMMY SPARKS

"*Doraemon* is a robot cat from the future who plays with kids like us," said Ethan.

ネコ型 ロボット『ドラえもん』も、アメリカでよく知られているよ」

"To satisfy growing demand, Japanese publishers supplied weekly magazines," said Dao. "Stores sold millions of copies. Editors explored new categories and topics to interest every reader."

「週かんで、発行されるまんがも、よく読まれているよ！へん集者は、読者がきょう味をもちそうな、新しいアイディアをいつもさがしているんだ」

Publishers targeted titles for males and females of all ages. Commuters read thick manga on the subway.

会社や学校に行く電車で、まんがを読んでいる人は、たくさんいる。 少年まんが、少女まんが、青年まんが、レディースコミックと、子どもざっしと、いろいろなまんが雑誌が、発行されている。

Seinen for men.

Josei for women.

Shōnen for boys.

Shōjo for girls.

There is even one for little children! (*kodomomuke*)

In the 1970s, the science-fiction genre of mecha featured giant machines. The teenager Koji pilots the 60-foot-tall *Mazinger* to protect the Earth.

1970年代には、ロボットアニメとよばれるジャンルが、登場する。 24メートルのきょ大な人型ロボット、マシンガーZをそうじゅうするのは、主人公の兜甲児 。 地球の平和を守るため、悪の力と戦うストーリー。

Gatchaman's five heroes drive vehicles that unite into a super plane.

『科学 忍者隊 ガッチャマン』は、5人の科学忍者隊の活 やくをかいた作品だ。

Mecha battled on other planets. *Space Battleship Yamato* recast Japan's grandest World War II ship into 2199.

『宇宙 戦艦 ヤマト』は、第二次 世界 大 戦 中 に、海にしずんだ戦艦「大和」を
宇宙船へと作り変え、2199年地球の平和を守るため、
銀 がけいの外へと旅立ち、い星人 との戦いに打ち勝っていくストーリー。

RK-78-2 GUNDAM

Boosted by popular toys, *Gundam* has spacecraft transform into huge armored samurais.

おもちゃや、プラモデルも大人気の『機動戦士 ガンダム』は、
モビルスーツといわれるガンダムロボットが、活やくする。

They leapt into the 1980s. "Women were creators too," said Ethan.

"Rumiko Takahashi spun funny stories about girls' relationships with boys," said Emma.

「1980年代には、女せい作家も出てきたよ」と、イーサン。
「高橋 留美子 は、ラブコメディをよくテーマにしたのよね」と、エマ。

"Meanwhile, *Dragon Ball* showed epic battles
of mythic warriors," noted Dao.

「『ドラゴンボール』は、ぼうけん、バトル、
友じょうをえがいた長へんまんがだよ」と、ダオ。

Other futuristic manga like *Akira* and *Ghost in the Shell* became anime. Translated into foreign languages, these thrilling and explosive adventures were unlike anything most Westerners had seen and made them want more.

『AKIRA』や、『攻殻機動隊』といったSFコミックは、えい画にもなって大ヒットし、英語やフランス語などに、やくされて世界中で高くひょうかされた。

1989 ended an era as both Japan's Emperor and Osamu Tezuka died.
But by then Hayao Miyazaki started a new one. His company Studio Ghibli
produced a string of celebrated animated movies, like *My Neighbor Totoro*.

1989年には、昭和 の時代が終わり、手塚も同年なくなった。その後、スタジオジブリの 宮崎 駿 は、
『となりのトトロ』をはじめ、多くのアニメをせい作した。

TOTORO

PRINCESS MONONOKE

MORO

NO-FACE

MEI

SATSUKE

BOH

CHIHIRO

Character labels in illustration:
PORCO ROSSO
KIKI
JIJI
NAUSICAÄ
SOSUKE
HOWL'S MOVING CASTLE
OHMU
PONYO

Exploring how people coexist with nature, his tales paint extraordinary lands in bold watercolors. Box office champs in Japan, they won awards worldwide and Miyazaki was called the "Walt Disney of Japan."

宮崎の作品は、自然との共生をテーマにしたものも多くある。また『千と千尋の神隠し』は、日本歴代こう行しゅう入第一位（2018年調べ）を記録している。国内だけでなく、アカデミー賞など世界中で多くの賞を受賞していて、宮崎は、「日本アニメーション界のディズニー」とよばれている。

In the 1990s, other stories gained fans around the globe. In *Sailor Moon*, teenage girls use magical powers as Earth's protectors. Cute characters, colored hair, pointed chins, and big eyes symbolized the *manga* style.

1990年代には、少女まんが『美 少女 戦士 セーラームーン』の連さいが始まり、
あっという間に大人気に。連さいと同じ時期に、テレビアニメ化されて世界中で大ヒットした。

SAILOR MOON

MARS

JUPITER

MERCURY

VENUS

"Originally a handheld video game, *Pokémon* jumped to trading cards, television, and then comics," marveled Dao.

「ポケモンは、もともとゲームボーイ用のソフトだったんだよ」と、ダオが、言った。「その後、テレビアニメ、キャラクター商品、カードゲームと、いろいろな形で登場し、世界中で人気が、出たんだ。

CHARIZARD

ASH KETCHUM

EEVEE

MEW

TOTODILE

PIKACHU

"Soon hundreds of creatures were found on books, home video, movies, dolls, merchandise, and clothing."

今では、800種類 をこえるポケモンがいるよ」

"40% of Japan's print sales was manga," said Dao.
"The *tankōbon* was the handiest way to buy and read."

Emma said, "Every Japanese spent an average of $50 a year!"

「日本では、まんがの年間はん売数は、出ぱん物全体の
約40パーセントをしめているんだ。まんがは、ざっしや、単行本など、
いろいろなかたちで読むことが、できるよ」と、ダオ。

エマは、「日本人は、一年に一人あたり、だいたい
50ドルをまんがに使っているんだって」と、びっくり。

Ethan said, "That's
a super fan, an *otaku*!"

「そんなに！まんがが大すきな人を、
まんがおたくっていうんだよね」
と、イーサン。

"Who's that?" asked Emma, noticing a shy girl scribbling in a sketchbook.

「あれは、だれ?」エマは、スケッチブックに絵をかいている少女を見つけた。

"Hmm... I don't know.
Not yet, anyway," answered Dao.
"She has *dōjinshi*... 'fan-fiction' stories
she made all by herself."

「えーっと、わからないな。少なくとも、今はね」と、ダオが、
答えた。「同人しを作っているみたいだね」

"Manga and anime can be about anything," noted Emma. "Pirates, ninjas, and kittens!"

「どんなものでも、まんがやアニメにできるのよね。海ぞくとか、にん者とか。あっ、ねこだって！」

MONKEY
D. LUFFY

NARUTO
UZUMAKI

EDWARD
ELRIC

SAITAMA

ALICIA
RUE

"Cat fangs, sweat drops, speed lines,
sparks, hearts, and eyes show
how a character feels," added Dao.

「あせマーク、人や物が動いたあとの線、スピード感を出す線、火花、
ハートマーク、気もちの変化を伝える目なんかを使って、
紙の上のキャラクターを生き生きと、えがき出すんだよ」と、ダオ。

"These are cool emoji!" joked Ethan.

「おもしろいね！」と、イーサンは、とても楽しそう。

Whoosh! They returned to the 21st century.
"Anime music is so catchy," sighed Emma.

ビューン！ダオと二人は、21世紀へ帰ってきた。
「アニメって音楽もすてきよね」と、エマ。

"Others admire the art," smiled Ethan. They toured
museums about creators, studios, and comics. "Now Japanese
creations influence artists and entertainment all over the globe."

「絵もとってもきれいだよね」と、イーサン。　二人は、原作者、せい作スタジオ、まんがをテーマにした
博物館めぐりをしている。「日本のまんがは、海外のアーティストや、
エンターテイメント業界 からすごく注目されているんだよ」

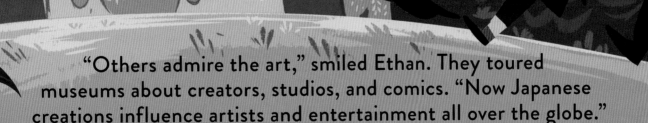

They were back in Tokyo, where stores overflowed with stories and streets with fans. "Today we can enjoy manga wherever we are," said Emma.

"Anime stream on the internet to TVs, computers, and phones," said Ethan.

東京にもどってきた。「今は、どこにいても、まんがを楽しめるわ。動画 配信 サービスって便利 よね」と、エマ

"We've come a long way!" concluded Emma.

"But it still starts with a good idea and elbow grease," added Ethan.

「まんがやアニメのこと、いろいろわかったわ」

「ずばぬけた発想と、地道な努力が、大切だね」

「あっ、そろそろ行かないと」
ダオは、ドラを鳴らした。ゴーン！

"Oops! That reminds me," yelped Dao. "It's time we go back."
He hit his gong. Gooone!

In a final puff of magic smoke, they were back at the Comic Con.
As the kids sorted their snazzy souvenirs, curious cosplayers gathered round.
"Was learning about anime and manga fun?" asked Dao.

ま法の、けむりに包まれて、コンベンションセンターへと帰ってきた。
まだ、ゆめ見心地のエマとイーサンの周りは、
コスプレをした人たちで、にぎわっている。

「楽しかったかい?」と、ダオ。

"You bet!" Ethan and Emma were inspired.
"We're going to write and draw our own cartoons!"

With a wiggle of his ears and a graphic novel in his paws,
Dao laughed, "I can't wait to read and watch them!"

「うん、すごく楽しかった！」「よーし、ぼくたちも、
まんがをかくぞ！」と、はりきる二人。

「早く読みたいな」と、
え顔でダオが、言った。

GLOSSARY

Anime animated programming originating from Japan.

Comic Con a comic book convention.

Cosplay blend of the words "costume" and "play." Cosplayers dress up as their favorite characters.

Dōjinshi manga drawn by amateurs; comparable to fan-fiction.

Dragon Ball action-packed shōnen manga created by Akira Toriyama.

Doraemon a robot cat from the future, created by Fujiko Fujio (pen name of the team Hiroshi Fujimoto and Motoo Abiko).

Emoji emotion symbols with origins in Japan's *keitai* (cellphone) culture.

Etoki the act of explaining images, specifically on Buddhist scrolls.

Gatchaman a TV anime called *Battle of the Planets* in the USA; created by Tatsuo Yoshida.

Genre a category of art with distinctive content.

Gundam a mecha story where robot soldiers fight in outer space.

Hokusai a famous Japanese woodcut artist (1760-1849).

Josei manga aimed at women.

Kamishibai a form of telling stories with large pictures in a wooden box.

Kodomomuke manga made for young kids.

Manga comic books and graphic novels originating from Japan.

Mazinger a heroic giant robot character; created by Go Nagai.

Mecha a genre of anime and manga that features big robots.

Miyazaki, Hayao an acclaimed manga artist and anime director.

Ninja a secret "shadow" soldier in ancient Japan.

Otaku a very dedicated fan, such as of anime and manga.

Pokémon a media franchise. It stands for "pocket monsters."

Sailor Moon shōjo manga authored by Naoko Takeuchi.

Samurai a warrior in ancient Japan.

Seinen manga targeted at men.

Serial a chapter of manga in an anthology of several different stories.

Shōjo manga aimed at girls.

Shōnen manga produced for boys.

Takahashi, Rumiko a bestselling female creator of anime and manga.

Tankōbon a complete book of manga; digest-sized.

Tetsujin 28-go a giant robot called *Gigantor* in the USA; created by Mitsuteru Yokoyama.

Tezuka, Osamu a legendary creator of beloved manga and anime.